W9-DDJ-190

MAX AND THE SECRET SKUNK

by Janet Adele Bloss

cover art by Gabriel

inside illustration by Mel Crawford

*To my good friends and Swissy lovers
Liz and Dick Githens*

Published by Willowisp Press
801 94th Avenue North, St. Petersburg, Florida 33702

Copyright © 1994 by Willowisp Press,
a division of PAGES, Inc.

All rights reserved. No portion of this book may be reproduced, stored in a retrieval system, or transmitted, in any form or by any means, electronic, mechanical, photocopying, recording, or otherwise, without written permission from the publisher.

Printed in the United States of America

2 4 6 8 10 9 7 5 3 1

ISBN 0-87406-719-7

Before I could stop her, Mrs. Hines pulled the closet door open. Kevin Snead pointed into my closet and shouted, "A skunk!"

Mrs. Hines dropped her papers and screamed. Mrs. Snead shrieked. She staggered backward against Mr. Snead, who fell against my dad, who fell against my bookshelf, which fell on the floor.

Mom poked her head in my closet, then suddenly clapped her hand over her nose. CD came waddling out with his tail stuck straight up in the air. Twisting in the middle, he pointed his head and his bottom at us.

One

GERSHWIN *Zimmerman.*
What a name! Why would parents name their kid Gershwin Zimmerman? When you give a kid a name like that you can bet he's going to turn out to be weird.

I watched Gershwin as he stood in front of the class, with his short red hair, blue eyes, glasses, and freckles. He acted like he didn't mind being the new kid. He just smiled at everyone as if we were lucky to be in the same room with him—the same way the Queen of England smiles. Not that the Queen of England is a close personal friend of mine. I've just seen her on TV, smiling, like Gershwin Zimmerman.

Mrs. Grove, my sixth-grade teacher, said, "Class! Gershwin has moved to Springfield, Ohio, all the way from Pittsburgh, Pennsylvania."

My friend Tony Lopez whispered, "Cool!" He leaned across the aisle and poked me in the ribs. "Pittsburgh! That's where Karl Morgan was born."

Ray Zander, my other best friend, said, "I wonder if the new kid knows Morgan?"

"Not likely," I said.

As you can probably guess, Karl Morgan is a hero of ours. He plays third base for the Redbirds. I've watched him play a hundred times in Lakeside Stadium. That's the great thing about living in Springfield. You get to see a pro ball team with players like Morgan. He's played in five All-Star Games. He hit seven home runs one month even though he was injured. I know all his stats. He's the best!

Mrs. Grove was still standing in front of the room with the new red-headed boy. "Gershwin's father is opening up a business here in Springfield," she told us.

Gershwin Zimmerman smiled as if he'd just been called from the minor leagues into the majors. "That's right," he said. "We own a pet shop called Zimmerman's Zoo."

"Cute," I muttered under my breath. Usually I like Fridays, but I could see this one was going to be different.

"Would you like to tell us a little more about yourself?" Mrs. Grove asked.

The Gersh-man puffed out his chest. You'd have thought he'd just been chosen best player in the National League. "Dad moved here last weekend," he said. "Mom and I got here yesterday. We bought a big house with a swimming pool on Oak Street."

"Wow!" hissed Ray. "That's the street next to where we live. I know that house. It's practically a mansion!"

"He must be rich," whispered Tony.

I shrugged and made a very quiet noise with my tongue between my lips.

Zimmerman ran a hand across his red hair.

Probably he was checking for termites. Then he said, "My mom is a model. My dad, mom, and I lived in England for a while. Then we spent last summer in Switzerland."

All the girls in the class started oohing and ahing. Girls like to hear stuff like that. They think anyone who lives outside of Ohio is a big-time world traveler.

Gershwin shoved his hands in his pockets. "We fly to Austria to ski every winter," he added.

I rolled my eyes for the benefit of Tony and Ray. "Big deal," I muttered. "I took a bus to Cleveland once."

"Shhhh!" It was Linda Lane who was shushing me. She leaned forward on her desk, watching the new guy as if he were a cupcake with very thick frosting.

"I enjoy mountain climbing," Gershwin continued. "And I'm also interested in collecting rocks. I've collected rocks from each country and state that I've visited."

"I'd be interested in bouncing a rock off his

head," I muttered under my breath.

I admit I'm usually not a violent person. But listening to people brag makes me want to throw things. Hard things. With pointy edges.

Mrs. Grove patted Gershwin Zimmerman's shoulder. "My!" she exclaimed. "You've certainly visited a lot of places." She turned to face us. "Class," she said, "I hope that you all will join me in welcoming Gershwin to Cedar Park Middle School."

For a minute I thought that Gershwin was going to stand in front of the class all day, telling us about how he used to live in Africa, Australia, New York, Jupiter, and in a submarine on the bottom of the Atlantic Ocean. And about how he planned to run cross-country for the U.S.A. in the next Olympic games. And how he was personal best friends with the governor of Wyoming and the president of Botswana. Some people like to go on and on about how great they are. I was glad when he finally sat down.

All the girls in the class started whispering. If you ask me, they all wanted to marry Gershwin Zimmerman. Girls act goofy around new guys.

"Wow," Tony said, "he sure has done a lot of exciting things."

"Yeah," agreed Ray. "I've never even been out of Ohio."

"He moved into the house the Jacksons used to live in," Tony whispered. "It's the biggest house on Oak Street."

Maybe Tony and Ray wanted to marry him, too. It sure sounded like it.

I tore a piece of paper from my notebook. I popped it into my mouth and chewed. Then I rolled it up between my fingers and aimed for the back of Gershwin's red head.

"You better not, Max," Tony warned. "Remember, you already got detention last week."

"Oh, yeah. I forgot." I flicked the spit wad onto the floor.

Mrs. Grove stood by the chalkboard. "Class,"

11

she said, "we've got eighteen days left in April. As some of you may know, the first week in May is National Be Kind to Animals Week."

Gershwin's hand shot into the air.

"Yes?" Mrs. Grove asked.

"It's the 81st National Be Kind to Animals Week," Gershwin informed us. "My father told me that. He knows about animals because of the pet shop we own."

Mr. Know-it-all was at it again.

Mrs. Grove looked surprised. "Thank you, Gershwin," she said. "In honor of Be Kind to Animals Week, we're going to have a contest with prizes."

Prizes? Here was something worth listening to.

"We will have a newspaper reporter here to take pictures of the winners," Mrs. Grove said. "Their pictures will be in the local newspaper."

"Cool!" I exclaimed. Ray, Tony, and I glanced excitedly at each other. It wasn't every day that a guy got his name and picture in the paper—

unless he was Karl Morgan with a World Series record.

"What's the contest about?" I asked.

"Each student in the class will write a report for National Be Kind to Animals Week," Mrs. Grove explained. "You may write about a pet if you have one. For those of you without pets, you may write about any animal you choose. A prize will be given to the student who writes the best report. Another prize will be given to the student with the most interesting pet. Those two students will receive ribbons and will have their photos in the newspaper."

The whole class began talking at the same time.

"A picture in the newspaper? Cool!" Linda Lane exclaimed. "I've got a guinea pig I can enter in the contest!"

"I'll write about my box turtle," said Scott Avery. "Man! My parents would flip if I got my picture in the paper!"

"I've got a cat," Pete Braisedell said.

Ray had a German shepherd named Bart. Tony had two beagles named Bruno and Crash. Everyone had a pet. Everyone but me.

Suddenly I didn't feel so hopeful. There was no way that I could win the Pet Contest. I was probably the only kid in the whole state of Ohio who didn't have a pet—not even an ant farm.

My only chance was to choose an interesting animal to write a report about. All kinds of animals galloped and hopped through my brain—giraffes, kangaroos, and zebras. Whatever animal I chose to write a report on, it would have to be an interesting one. Otherwise there was no way I would win the report contest.

Mrs. Grove gave us more details about the contest. She said, "You may bring your pets to class to show to the other students. Or you may bring a picture of your pet. If you bring your pet, it must be in a cage. Or a parent may bring the animal to school for you. When all of the reports have been given and all of the pets have been seen, we will vote for whomever we think has the most interesting pet and the best report. You students will choose the winners. I've posted a report schedule on the wall. When the bell rings, check to see on what day you will give your report."

Tony leaned across the aisle. "Maybe I can teach Bruno and Crash some tricks," he said. "Beagles are really smart. I'll bet the pet who knows the most tricks will win the contest."

"Forget it, dude," said Ray. "Bart's got it in the bag. My dog is bigger and can run faster than your dogs. I think that the biggest and strongest pet will win the contest."

Suddenly they got real quiet. Tony and Ray looked at me as if I'd just been told I had twenty-four hours to live. In a way, that's how I felt.

"Sorry about your sister's allergies, Max," Ray said. "Too bad you don't have a pet."

He might as well have said, "Too bad you don't have a head." That's what I felt like. It was just like my dumb older sister, Tiffany, to ruin everything.

"Oh, well," I said, "I can still write a report."

Just then the bell rang. Everyone jumped up and ran to check the pet report schedule.

I pushed my way through the crowd. Scanning down the list, I saw that Ray and Linda Lane were giving their reports on the same day. Then there was Tony and Scott Avery, Pete Braisedell and Mark Harris, and Bev Daily and Marilyn McConahay. Some of the kids wrote their pets beside their names:

LINDA LANE—*guinea pig, Snowball*
RAY ZANDER—*German shepherd, Bart*
TONY LOPEZ—*beagles, Bruno and Crash*
SCOTT AVERY—*box turtle, Tank*

But where was my name?

I could hardly believe my eyes when, at last, I saw my name. There it was on the very last day of the reports:

<u>Friday</u>
MAX WASHINGTON
GERSHWIN ZIMMERMAN

16

It was just my luck to be paired with the new dork in town. Out of the corner of my eye I saw a flash of red hair. Gershwin Zimmerman was standing next to me. He reached out with a pen and wrote beside his name:

Greater Swiss mountain dog,
Mr. Mighty Johann

I should have known that the Zimmer-man wouldn't have a hamster or a goldfish. It was just like him to have the kind of pet that a movie star would probably own.

Linda Lane was looking at Gersh and acting goofy. "What kind of dog is a Greater Swiss mountain dog?" she giggled.

"It's very rare and expensive," Gershwin explained. "You pronounce the *j* in Johann like a *y*. That's how the Swiss say it. Mr. Mighty Johann is his registered name. He's a show dog. He cost one thousand dollars."

"Awesome!" exclaimed Linda. "My guinea pig was only twenty bucks."

"Not many people know about Swissies," Gershwin said. "There are four kinds of Swiss mountain dogs. The Greater Swiss is the biggest one. Mr. Mighty Johann weighs 130 pounds. He can knock down a full-sized man."

If anyone got knocked down, I wished it would be Gersh. He kept on blabbing and bragging.

"I'll probably win the contest," Gersh continued. "Swissies are cool dogs. They're strong enough to live in the Alps. Those are mountains in Switzerland, in case you didn't know." Gersh probably thought none of us had ever had a geography lesson.

The Gersh-meister went on. "I've had my picture in the paper before with Mr. Mighty Johann. He won the best of breed at the Eastern Regional Specialty Show two years in a row."

"Your dog has won a professional contest against other show dogs?" asked Linda.

"Twice," said Gersh.

"Gee," said Linda, "you're probably right about winning the contest. You might even win *both* of the prizes—for the most interesting pet *and* for the best report."

Gershwin nodded. "I might. Swissies are good-looking dogs. They've got short hair, mostly black, with a white chest and muzzle, tan legs, and floppy ears. They're very strong dogs," he said. "You'll see that when I bring Mr. Mighty to class."

"Are they stronger than German shepherds?" asked Ray.

"About ten times stronger," said Gershwin.

"Are they smarter than beagles?" asked Tony.

"Mr. Mighty has been to obedience school," said Gershwin. "He can sit, come, stay, speak, heel, and roll over."

"Can he write my English report for me?" I muttered.

Gershwin shot me a glance as he pushed his glasses up his nose.

"Gosh," Marilyn said. "We might as well give Gershwin both prizes right now. Nobody in our class has a pet as good as his."

"I do!" I said.

The words popped out of my mouth before I had time to stop them. Ray and Tony looked at me as if I were nuts, because they knew the closest thing to a pet I had were the flies that buzzed around my gym shoes in the summer.

Gershwin stared at me. "You? What kind of pet do you have?" he asked. "Is it better than a Greater Swiss mountain dog?"

"Much better," I said. I felt the sweat begin to drip down my neck.

Gershwin frowned. "What kind of pet do you have?" he asked again.

I had to think fast.

"It's a secret," I said. My heart was pounding. "I can't tell you right now. But it's a hundred times better than a Swiss mountain goat."

"Swiss mountain dog," Zimmerman corrected me.

"What is it, Max?" asked Linda curiously.

"Yeah, what kind of great pet do you have?" asked Bev.

"What have you got?" asked Scott.

They all stared at me suspiciously.

"You'll find out soon enough," I said, trying to sound mysterious.

I rushed from the classroom into the hall. Ray and Tony pressed close beside me. "You're in deep yogurt now, dude," Ray said.

I stuck a finger under the collar of my T-shirt to let the steam out. Gershwin walked right by me with Linda Lane, Scott Avery, and some of the other kids in our class. It was his first day at our school and already he was acting like he owned the place.

I heard Gershwin say, "Wait until you see my dog. He's a champion. Nobody can beat him! Nobody!" he said, with a glance in my direction.

I needed a pet, and I needed one fast.

21

Two

IT was Saturday. I'd had all night and morning to work up the courage to ask my parents about getting a pet. "We wouldn't have to get a big dog," I pleaded. "Just a little one."

Mom and Dad stared at me.

"A cat?" I asked. "A tiny cat? With no fur? A bald cat? Without a tail? We could shave his whiskers off."

I was desperate. Dad just shook his head. "Tiffany has allergies," he reminded me.

"You know how your sister gets around animals," Mom said. "Her eyes swell up and her nose drips. She has to take antihistamines."

Those are pills that my sister takes for

allergies. My mom is a nurse. She knows all about that stuff. I thought about Tiffany. It was just my luck to have a sister who was allergic to fur. Why couldn't she have been allergic to staying in the bathroom all day? Or allergic to watching barfy love movies on TV?

The front door opened. Tiffany rushed in with a big box under her arm. "Oh, Mother!" she shrieked. "I picked up the hat I'm wearing in Heather's wedding. It's beautiful!"

My sister was going to be a bridesmaid in our cousin Heather's wedding. She'd been talking about it for weeks. She was proud that at fifteen years old, she would be the youngest bridesmaid in the wedding. Big deal.

Tiffany ripped open the top of the box and pulled out a hat. It was a huge thing that looked like an explosion in a flower shop. Tiffany stuck it on her head. She danced around the room like a maniac. Ribbons and flowers bounced on her brides-dork hat.

"Oh, honey. That's lovely!" Mom said.

"Is your dress ready yet?"

"Not quite," Tiffany said.

I turned to my dad. He was my only hope. "Please," I begged. "I really need a pet. It's for a school report. Everyone else has a dog or a cat or *something*."

Tiffany stopped whirling. She glared at me from under the fake flowers. "A pet?" she asked. "You want to bring a dirty animal in this house? I'd never be able to breathe," she moaned, clutching her throat.

"You'd get used to it," I said. "Please, Tiff. Wouldn't you like to have a dog?"

"Dogs stink," said Tiffany.

"A cat?" I asked hopefully.

"Cats have fleas," said Tiffany.

Turning to mom, she said, "You're not going to let him get a pet, are you?" She touched her nose. "Remember my allergies?"

Mom nodded. "I remember, Tiffany," she said. Mom sighed deeply, patted my back, and said, "Sorry, Max, I'm afraid it's out of the question."

Dad looked concerned. I'd told him all about the report for school. "Couldn't you borrow someone else's pet?" he asked. "Just take it to school on report day?"

"It's not the same," I said. I thought about all the kids in my class and how they'd heard me say that I had a secret pet. If I didn't come up with one, I'd be branded forever as the biggest liar in the sixth grade.

And what about Gershwin Zimmerman, the new weirdo in our class? He thought he had everything—a swimming pool, ski trips, a rock collection, a pet shop, and a Greater Swiss mountain dog. He'd been in our class for five minutes and already he was bragging about winning the pet contest and the report contest.

Tiffany took the jungle off her head and stuck it back in the box. "You can't have a pet," she said, sniffing. "I won't have my nose swelling up before Heather's wedding. How can I walk down the aisle if my eyes swell shut? How would I look?"

"Like a dork," I agreed.

Dad sighed. "Max, how about getting some goldfish? Your sister's not allergic to goldfish."

A goldfish didn't stand a chance against a Greater Swiss mountain dog.

I shook my head and left the room. What else was there to do? I left the house and walked across the backyard to my treehouse. My Dad and I built it together. It's my hideaway, the place I go when everyone else is acting goofy.

I climbed the rungs up the side of the tree and pulled myself through the trap door. Then I hoisted the green flag up on a pole on the rooftop. The green flag means that I'm in the treehouse. It's a sign for Ray and Tony to come over if they're not doing anything. We live near each other, so they can see the flag if they ride by on their bikes.

I lay down on the treehouse floor, careful not to get poked by any of the nail heads that needed to be hammered down. Thoughts of my sister floated through my mind. Most of the thoughts were about how I'd like to take a lawn mower to her stupid wedding hat. Then I thought about how I'd let Tiffany live in the treehouse—free of charge—if I could move a dog into her bedroom. A big dog with lots of fur.

I thought about Karl Morgan, and I wondered if he had pets when he was my age. I'll bet he did. He seemed like the kind of guy who probably had a pony and a couple of dogs. He probably never had a fifteen-year-old sister, either.

"Yo, Max!"

"Hey, dude!"

It was Tony and Ray. I opened the trap door and let them in as they climbed up.

"Wow!" exclaimed Tony. "I just walked by Zimmerman's house. I looked through the fence. Man, that pool is giant!"

"That's some house," Ray agreed. "His old man must have a serious bank account."

"Did you see his champion dog?" I asked.

"Nope." Ray shook his head.

"Didn't see anyone," said Tony. "Hey, that's

a cool contest Mrs. Grove talked about yesterday. Everyone thinks Zimmerman is going to win. His dog has already won contests against other show dogs. Too bad we don't stand a chance of winning it."

"I can win it if I teach Bart a new trick," insisted Ray. "We're going to work on one where I put a piece of bologna on my top lip, under my nose. Then Bart eats it."

"Zimmerman's dog has been to college," I said sarcastically. "I don't think the bologna trick is going to work."

But at least he had a dog to enter in the contest. Without a pet I didn't even stand a chance on the pet part of the contest.

Tony shrugged his shoulders. "Crash and Bruno don't know many tricks. Maybe I can get a prize for the worst-smelling pets."

I had to laugh at that.

"What's all this 'secret pet' stuff?" asked Ray, looking at me. "Do you really have one?"

I shook my head. "I thought about entering

my sister in the contest. But I figured that Mr. Mighty Johann is probably better trained than she is."

Ray and Tony laughed.

"Everyone at school is wondering what kind of pet you're entering," said Tony, turning to me.

"Gershwin asked me what kind of pet you have," said Ray.

"What did you tell him?" I asked.

"I told him I was sworn to secrecy."

Good old Ray. I knew I could count on him. Ray, Tony, and I had been friends since first grade. We grew up in Springfield together. We'd been to a hundred Redbirds games together, and eaten a thousand hot dogs, and tons of peanuts at Lakeside Stadium. We sent Karl Morgan a get-well card when he hurt his right ankle. Even with ankle and back problems, Morgan tied for first on the team in homers with 18. I think that the three of us knew more about Karl Morgan than any other kids in Ohio. We were sort of a private fan club for Karl.

"What are you going to do when you have to bring your pet to school?" asked Ray.

"I don't know," I moaned.

Tony looked at his watch. "I've gotta run," he said. "Mom's taking me to the mall for some school supplies."

"The mall?" I echoed. Suddenly I had an idea. "Isn't there a pet shop at the mall?" I asked.

"There used to be," said Tony.

"Maybe I could buy a pet!" I said.

"What about your parents?" Ray asked.

I felt a pang of conscience jab at me. But I ignored it. "I'll get something little," I said. "Something I can hide in my room. They'll never know."

"What about your sister's allergies?" asked Tony.

"I'll get . . . something bald!" I said. "They're bound to have something without fur."

I breathed deeply. Suddenly it seemed as if I might have a chance of winning the contest after all. I admit it was sneaky to go behind my parents' back. But if they'd known how much having a pet meant to me, they'd have understood. After all, they wouldn't want their kid to have a reputation as the biggest liar in the sixth grade, would they? The family honor was at stake.

Mom gave me permission to go to the mall with Tony. His mom drove us. Ray came along. While Mrs. Lopez was doing some shopping, we walked down to where the pet shop used to be. There was a new sign in the front window: ZIMMERMAN'S ZOO.

"Oh, no!" I groaned. "This is the pet shop that Gershwin's dad owns." I peeked in through the front window. I didn't see Gershwin.

With my life savings in my pocket ($15.47), I walked into the store. First I checked out the puppies. A Boston terrier was $250. There was a Dalmatian puppy for $300. I couldn't believe the prices. Even the kittens were $25. No wonder Gershwin had to be rich.

A sales clerk came. I told her that I had $15.47 and wanted a pet. I said I'd take anything

I could afford, except for fish. She thought about it. "We're having a special on gerbils," she said. "Two for one. And there's a damaged cage on sale."

"Are any of your gerbils bald?" I asked.

The lady looked at me like I was nuts.

I thought about Tiffany and her allergies. How could anyone be allergic to something as small as a gerbil? The sale on gerbils was too good to pass up even if they weren't bald.

I got to thinking that maybe I could teach those little guys some really excellent tricks. Maybe I could train the world's smartest gerbils. Then my pets would run circles around Mr. Mighty Johann.

I guess in my heart I knew that a dog was a better pet than a gerbil. But when all you've got is $15.47 in your pocket and you're desperate, you can talk yourself into believing anything.

"You wait and see," I promised Tony and Ray. "These little guys will make all the other pets look like morons! I'll write a super report about them, too. I'll win *both prizes!*"

Ray snorted with laughter. "We'd better get out of here. The fumes are getting to Max."

I got some dry food, paid, and left the shop carrying the gerbil cage with its two gerbils. They looked scared as they huddled together in the wood shavings. I stopped for a moment to look more closely at them. The bigger one wiggled his nose at me. "Hulk," I said. "That's your name."

Then the smaller one, his buddy, jumped up into the wheel and began running. The exercise wheel squeaked as it whirled around. "That one is Gizmo," I said. "Hulk and Gizmo." I peered closely at them. "Listen, guys," I said, "you've got to help me win this contest. Okay?"

Gizmo kept running in the wheel. He didn't seem to hear a thing I said. Hulk cleaned his front paws.

"I'll show that Gershwin Zimmerman a thing or two," I muttered.

"Sure you will," said Ray. "Revenge of the gerbils!" He smothered a laugh behind his hand.

Sneaking the gerbils into the house wasn't easy. I waited until I saw Mom, Dad, and Tiffany through the living room window. Then I ran to the backyard and came through the kitchen door. With my jacket draped over the cage, I tiptoed up to my room. Then I yelled downstairs to let Mom know I was home.

A moment later, Mom called, "Dinner's ready!"

"You guys go in the closet for now," I said to Hulk and Gizmo. Already I liked them. They were the first pets I'd ever had, except for a frog I caught one summer at camp.

I put food in their cage and put them in my closet with my flashlight on so they wouldn't be in the dark. Then I walked downstairs to the dinner table. Tiffany sat across from me.

"Ah-choo!" she sneezed, just the way she does when there's an animal nearby. Tiff grabbed a dinner napkin and held it to her nose. "Ah-choo!" Her eyes were beginning to turn pink around the edges—sort of like a gerbil's.

Three

MY sister sneezed a lot all weekend. She took extra antihistamine pills. Lucky for me she never came into my room. If she had she probably would have sneezed her head off.

Gizmo woke me up on Monday morning by running around in his wheel. I could hear it squeaking in the closet. I jumped out of bed and opened my closet door.

"Shhhh!" I warned him. "Do you want to get us caught?"

I gave Hulk and Gizmo a handful of sunflower seeds. They sat up on their hind legs and held the seeds in their forepaws. Their noses and whiskers twitched as they nibbled.

"Don't you worry, little guys," I whispered. "I'm going to train you to do some great tricks. We'll show Mr. Know-it-all Zimmerman who has the best pet!"

Hulk flicked his tail and ran his paw over his ear. It was almost like he was saluting me, saying, "Yes, sir, Captain."

"Max! Breakfast is ready!" Mom called up the stairs.

I quickly closed my closet door and finished getting dressed. Monsters stared down at me from the posters on my walls as I pulled my shoes on. The monster posters guarded my room from my dork sister. Tiffany couldn't stand to look at the posters, especially the one of the Headless Warrior, so she never came in my room. That meant that Hulk and Gizmo were safe from my nosy sister.

I hurried downstairs to the kitchen. Mom had on her white nurse's uniform that she wears to work at the hospital. Dad had already gone to work at the insurance office. Tiffany was still in the bathroom, probably putting a ton of makeup on to hide her zits.

After breakfast I walked down to the corner, like I did every morning. Ray and Tony were waiting for me.

"Yo, Max!" said Tony. "What's happening?"

"Did you start your pet report yet?" asked Ray.

I shook my head no.

Ray showed us a scratch on his neck from where he spent the weekend trying to teach his dog, Bart, to eat a piece of bologna from his ear. Ray was pretty serious about winning the pet contest. I warned Ray that he might lose a piece of his face if he wasn't careful with his bologna tricks.

The bell rang just as we got to school. We hurried to Mrs. Grove's room. Gershwin was sitting at his desk. He looked at me as I ran to get into my seat before the second bell. I'll bet Gershwin Zimmerman has never been late for a class in his life.

The morning went by okay. Mrs. Grove talked about adding decimal numbers in math class. Then we had science class, where we learned about the different parts of a worm. Real useful stuff. If you ever need to know something about a worm, just ask me.

The hours went by and at last it was time for lunch. Monday is pizza day—the one day of the week where the cafeteria cooks don't try to poison us. I sat at a table with Ray and Tony. We munched on our pizza.

With a mouthful of pepperoni, Ray asked, "Do you think Morgan will make the All-Star team again this year?"

"I don't know," I said. "He's done it five times. He can probably do it again."

The girls at our table were whispering to each other. They always ignore us when we talk about baseball. That's one reason we talk about it.

Someone put a lunch tray beside mine on the table. Looking up, I was surprised to see Gershwin Zimmerman. He pulled out a chair and sat down. All the girls started giggling like maniacs.

Linda Lane smiled her phoniest smile. "Do you really think you'll win the pet contest, Gershwin?" she asked.

"Of course!" he answered. "What pet could be more interesting than a Greater Swiss mountain dog?" He picked the pieces of pepperoni off his pizza and folded them into his napkin, as if they were poison mushrooms.

"Where did you get such a cool dog?" asked Bev Daily.

"In Switzerland," Gersh replied. "We lived there for a summer. We bought Mr. Mighty Johann from a dog breeder. He comes from a long line of champions. His mother was TriSatin Cadmir of Berne. His father was Cashmere Redmond Von Oland."

"His cousin was John Jacob Jingleheimer Schmidt," I whispered to Ray, who practically choked on his pizza.

The Gersh-man shot us a dirty look. He

ignored me and kept talking. "Swissies are good at herding, guarding, and pulling carts," he said. "They're strong and brave. If people get caught in an avalanche of snow in the mountains, a Swissy can find them, pull them out, and save their lives."

I looked at my dessert and wondered if Gersh would like to be in an avalanche of cherry cobbler.

It was time to get back to a good conversation. "Did your dad get tickets for the next game?" I asked Ray. "They're playing St. Louis."

"Twenty-second row. Behind the Redbirds' dugout," Ray said proudly.

"What's Morgan's average?" Tony asked.

".333," I said.

"What's so great about Karl Morgan?" asked Linda Lane.

"Are you serious?" I asked. "One year he led the league with thirty-three doubles. He's made the top 10 in stolen bases, extra base hits, total bases, multi-hit games, and slugging percentage. He leads the National League in third basemen fielding. When he was a Redbirds rookie he stole more bases than anyone since 1909. He represented the Redbirds on a Major League All-Star tour of Japan. He set a World Series fielding record for third basemen in the World Series versus Oakland."

Linda looked bored.

"I think last year was his best year," said Ray.

"Maybe," I agreed. "Thirty-two homers, 92 RBIs, and 182 hits. He led the Redbirds in games, at-bats, and runs. The guy can do no wrong. He's fantastic!"

"You don't think he'll be traded to any other team, do you?" asked Ray.

"Not if the Redbirds know what's good for them," I said.

Tony commented, "The Springfield Redbirds without Karl Morgan is like . . . like . . . "

"Pizza without pepperoni," I said, glancing at Gershwin's napkin.

"Karl Morgan's a nice guy," said Gershwin. He looked from me to Ray to Tony. "We had him over to dinner once when we lived in Pittsburgh. That's where Morgan's from."

As if I didn't already know that.

"My Dad knows him. Mr. Morgan had dinner with us." The Zimmer-man smiled. "His wife, Lucy, and daughter, Julie, came, too."

He said it like it was the most normal thing in the world to have the greatest baseball player in the universe in your home.

"Give me a break!" I exclaimed. "Your dad knows Karl Morgan? Not likely!"

Gershwin's eyebrows shot up. "Sure he does," he insisted. "And I've met him twice. I helped him wax his car once."

"No way!" I said. "Somebody give this guy some oxygen. He's hallucinating!"

Linda Lane leaned her elbows onto the table. "Do you really know a famous baseball player?" she asked.

"Of course," said Gershwin. "I've got an

43

autographed baseball to prove it."

"You've got a baseball autographed by Karl Morgan?" asked Ray. His chin was practically hanging down to his lunch tray.

Gershwin nodded. "My dad knows Morgan because my grandfather used to work with Morgan's dad at the Pittsburgh Postal Service. My grandfather and Karl's dad were both mailmen. His mom was a waitress."

I could hardly believe what I was hearing. Here was this guy who spent the first part of lunch bragging about his expensive dog. Now he was bragging about how he knew Karl Morgan. And that he had an autographed baseball from him!

It was too much. It couldn't be true, could it?

"Karl likes spaghetti," said Gershwin. "That's what we had for dinner the night he came over."

"Gee," said Bev. "You sure have an interesting family. It must be neat to know someone famous, and to own a pet store, and to have a dog from Switzerland." She shook her head.

"Maybe I shouldn't enter my cat in the contest. Fluffy doesn't stand a chance against your dog. No one's pet does."

Suddenly all eyes turned toward me. I could tell everyone was thinking about what I'd said the Friday before about my "secret pet" who was a hundred times better than a Greater Swiss mountain dog. My ears began to feel warm. They tend to do that whenever I wish I were someplace else—like in another solar system.

Gershwin stared at me. "Maxwell claims he has a great pet," he said.

I hate it when people call me Maxwell.

"Will you give us a clue as to what your pet is?" Gershwin winked at the girls and they began to laugh.

"A hint? Pass the *cheese*, please," said Ray. A grin tugged at the corners of his mouth.

I noticed that Tony's nose was twitching up and down, like a gerbil's.

I kicked my two friends under the table.

"Ow!" yelled Tony.

"No clues," I said. "You'll have to find out on Pet Day."

I was glad when the bell rang. I spent the rest of the day thinking about that baseball autographed by Karl Morgan and about Gershwin's expensive, rare dog. Thinking about it made me feel like my life was boring. Was it really possible for a boy like Gershwin to have so many adventures, while I had none?

I began thinking about the pet contest. I admit Hulk and Gizmo weren't much of a match for a Greater Swiss mountain dog. But they were all I had. I became more determined than ever to teach them some tricks. I once saw a trained mouse run up a guy's arm and down his shoulder, take a piece of cheese from his shirt pocket, and climb up and sit on top of his head. I'd like to see a Swiss mountain dog do that!

I stayed up late that night after school. Mom, Dad, and Tiff were asleep. Little did they

time I put them back in the closet. It was late. I felt good about my new pets. Maybe, just maybe, they'd have a chance in the pet contest. I mean, how many people have trained gerbils?

I slid into bed and was asleep in two minutes. I dreamed I was in a giant cheese sandwich. That's probably because I forgot to take some cheese out of my pajama pocket.

It seemed like five minutes later when Mom knocked on my door and told me to get up for school.

I climbed slowly out of bed and pulled my clothes on. I opened my closet door and pulled out the cage to give Hulk and Gizmo some seeds for breakfast.

Then I looked closer. There were the wood shavings on the cage floor. There was the exercise wheel and the water bottle.

But where were the gerbils? They were gone!

Four

"I guess I didn't close the cage door," I moaned to Ray and Tony. We were in the locker room getting ready for Tuesday gym class. "Just my luck. The only pets I've ever had—and they've already escaped."

"Okay, boys," called Mr. Boyd, the gym coach. "Quit the chatter. Let's go!"

I laced up my gym shoes and ran into the gym. While we did push-ups, Mr. Boyd called out, "One-two-one-two!" It looked to me as if Mr. Boyd needed to do a few push-ups himself.

"Okay, boys," he called. "Let's practice our sprints. Zimmerman, you race Washington for the fifty-yard dash."

Gershwin got into position beside me. Looking up at the coach, he said, "I ran track back in Pittsburgh. I won several ribbons."

I felt my heart begin to pound faster. I'd show that bragging bag of bologna once and for all that he wasn't the best at everything.

Mr. Boyd blew his whistle. I bolted from the starting line. As I pumped my knees up and down, it felt as though my lungs were going to pop out of my mouth. I breathed hard as I ran. Out of the corner of my eye I could see red hair right beside me.

"You tied!" Mr. Boyd said as we crossed the finish line.

I breathed heavily, glad that I'd run my best race. Gersh wiped sweat from his forehead. "Darn!" he exclaimed. "I didn't run very well. My ankle still hurts from when I sprained it hang gliding."

Hang gliding? Was there *anything* this guy hadn't done?

Pete Braisedell came over and nudged me in

51

the ribs. "Hey, Max," he said, "I hear you have some kind of secret pet."

"That's right," I said. I didn't mention that my secret pets were lost somewhere in my house, probably with their noses squashed in one of my mother's mousetraps.

"Did Maxwell tell you what his pet is yet?" It was Gershwin Zimmerman who had joined the group.

"It's a secret," I said, trying not to sound nervous.

The Zimmer-man grinned. "Mr. Mighty Johann just got back from the groomers," he said. "His nails have been clipped. He's been washed and brushed. He looks as good as he did when he won his three 5-point majors at the Maryland Specialty."

"He sounds like a beauty contestant," I said. "What did he do for the talent part of the contest? Play the accordion?"

"Your dog will probably blow away the competition in our class pet contest," Pete said.

"That's right," Gersh said proudly.

Scott Avery spoke up. "Don't get too cocky, Gersh," he warned. "Remember, Max has a secret pet."

"Yeah!" exclaimed Pete. "It better be good if it's going to beat Gersh's pet."

Everyone stared at me. "It's a great pet," I said, forcing a grin. Ray and Tony bugged their eyes out at me.

"Max's secret pet," said Gersh. "I wonder what it is."

"You'll find out," I said, then hurried away as the coach blew his whistle.

After showers and changing, we walked to our lockers. Ray asked, "What are you going to do? Everyone thinks you've got a great pet. Some of the kids think you're hiding an alligator in your basement."

"I wish," I said. I grabbed my books from my locker. We were walking home from school.

Ray walked to my house. As we came through the front door, I heard my sister yelling in her room. Mom came running out of the kitchen.

"Tiffany! What's wrong?" Mom called.

"Someone knocked my bath powder off my dresser!" Tiffany shouted.

You would have thought someone had mixed flea powder in with her bath powder, for all the noise she was making.

Ray and I followed Mom to Tiff's bedroom. She was wearing her brides-dork hat, the one with the flowers all over it. It looked weird with her jeans.

Her powder box was overturned. A trail of white powder traced across the floor and disappeared under her bed. Little paw prints, like tiny hands, could be seen. Quickly, I covered the prints with my foot. It looked as if Hulk and Gizmo were alive and well—in my sister's bedroom.

"Did you do this?" Tiffany asked me accusingly. "Ah-choo!" She sneezed and rubbed her eyes.

"I haven't touched your powder," I said.

"Hmmm." Mom frowned and scratched her chin.

Ray and I left Tiff's room and went to my room. My monster posters grinned down at me. I showed Ray the empty gerbil cage in my closet. A moment, later, I heard Mom yell, "Max! Come here . . . immediately!"

It was her you're-in-trouble voice.

When Ray and I got to the kitchen, Mom was holding up a lemon meringue pie. There was a big hole in the meringue. It looked as if the pie had exploded.

"Did you eat this?" Mom asked. "Max, you know I've asked you not to pick at the desserts I bake. This was supposed to be for Mrs. Sammons. She just got home from the hospital."

I inspected the hole in the pie. It looked as if Hulk and Gizmo had raided the kitchen. Maybe they'd spent the day eating pie and rolling in my sister's powder. Not a bad life for a gerbil.

"I didn't touch your pie," I said.

"Hmm." Mom looked puzzled.

I figured this was a good time to get out of the house. It seemed that I was always the one who got blamed for everything. How come my sister was never accused of eating the tops off pies?

Ray and I went outside and climbed up into the tree house. We raised the green flag, then sat on the floor.

I said, "I'm glad Hulk and Gizmo are alive. I hope I can find them before the pet contest."

Ray belched loudly. It's something we try to do a lot of when we're in the tree house. I swallowed some air and beat his belch by a good two seconds.

Luckily I had eighteen days left to find a new pet for the contest since my report day was on a Friday. But what could I do? I didn't have any money left to buy a new pet. The only pets I had were running around the house raiding the kitchen and my sister's bedroom.

I sighed and leaned back against the wall, wondering what Karl Morgan would have done if he were in my shoes. Probably a guy who could hit homers in consecutive innings of a World Series game never had to worry about gerbils, sisters, and new dorks in school who bragged a lot.

There was a sudden sound on the ground outside. Lifting the trap door, I saw Tony climbing up the rungs. "Have I got good news for you!" he exclaimed. He pulled himself into the tree house. Then he snatched a piece of newspaper from his pocket.

"It's your secret pet!" he shouted. "The answer to all your problems! You'll win the contest for sure!"

I grabbed the newspaper clipping and read:

SKUNK
Free to good home

A skunk? That was worth ten Greater Swiss mountain dogs! Who would have a pet more interesting than a skunk? Who? Not even Gershwin Zimmerman! A skunk! It was the answer to my prayers!

Five

WE didn't waste any time. I told Mom I was going to ride my bike, which was true. Tony, Ray, and I jumped on our bicycles and took off, pedaling as fast as we could. We rode across town into a rundown neighborhood.

"Are you sure this is the place?" Ray asked.

"It's the address in the ad," I said, rechecking the newspaper.

Tony, Ray, and I jumped off our bicycles and stared at an apartment building. We looked at unit 12-A with its broken window and scratched door.

"Nice home for a skunk," said Ray.

We laid our bikes on the ground and walked

up to the front door. The mailbox had a name on it: E. Lawrence. A man with a beard answered my knock.

"Whaddaya want?" he asked. His big toe stuck through a hole in his sock.

"Mr. Lawrence? I came about the skunk," I said. "The *free* skunk."

Mr. Lawrence turned and disappeared into his apartment. A moment later he came back with a skunk in a cage. He opened the door and lifted the skunk out. The white stripe stretched from the skunk's head down his back and along his bushy, black tail. His body was about a foot long. He had claws, but they didn't look very sharp.

"This is CD," said Mr. Lawrence. "That's short for Captain Dink. He's had his rabies shots."

CD lay quietly in Mr. Lawrence's arms. The skunk stared at me with shiny brown eyes. A little blue collar was buckled around his neck.

"Cool!" said Tony.

Ray took a step backwards. "Will he spray us?" he asked.

"Nah," said Mr. Lawrence. "His musk gland was removed." He lifted the tail to show us. But I wasn't sure what a skunk musk gland looked like. So I don't know if I saw it or not.

CD blinked his eyes and poked his nose at Mr. Lawrence's chest.

"He's a friendly fella," said Mr. Lawrence. "I've had him since he was a baby. Most skunks act wild. Even when you've had them a long time. You never know what they're gonna do. But CD's not like that. He doesn't bite like other skunks."

"Why are you giving him away?" I asked.

The man shrugged. "People are funny about skunks," he said. "My landlord won't let me keep him. Do you have a place for him to stay?"

"Yeah," I said. "I'll take good care of him." I figured he'd be just fine in my bedroom closet.

"What does he eat?" I asked.

"Insects. Crickets, roaches, grasshoppers,

mice, frogs, eggs, baby birds, berries, grain, nuts, snakes, turtles, garbage. Skunks eat almost anything," he said. "He likes it outside," he added, handing me a leash. "He'll go for walks with you. Here's the cage." He handed it to Tony.

Mr. Lawrence gave the skunk to me. CD was lighter than he looked, about eight pounds. I held him in my arms. He started to squirm. I could tell CD wanted to go back to his old owner.

"He's a good little fella," Mr. Lawrence said, giving CD a pat on the head. "You take care of him," he added.

"I will," I promised.

Mr. Lawrence gave CD another pat on the head. Then he closed the door, leaving me outside with a skunk in my arms.

"Cool pet!" exclaimed Ray. "You'll win the pet contest for sure!"

I stroked CD's fur. "Let's go home, little guy," I said. Ray helped me put the skunk in my backpack. Tony strapped the cage to his handlebars and front fender with a bungee cord. Then we got on our bikes and began pedaling across town to our neighborhood.

As I pedaled along, I felt CD squirming on my back and scratching at the pack. I wondered how I could keep the skunk a secret from my family. If Tiffany's nose sneezed at gerbils, it would probably explode with a skunk in the house.

We turned onto Oak Street. My heart raced faster as I saw a red head in the distance.

"It's the Gersh-man!" I exclaimed.

He was walking alone on the sidewalk in front of his house. I looked around to see if his dog was nearby. But there was no sign of the great, expensive, champion Mr. Mighty Johann.

As we rode our bikes past Gersh, I could tell that he was staring at the empty cage on Tony's bike. He would have blown a gasket if he'd known what was in my backpack.

By the time we got to my house, CD was starting to make hissing sounds.

We hopped off our bikes in the backyard. Suddenly it all seemed impossible.

"I can't take him in the house," I admitted. "My parents will find him. He's too big to hide like a gerbil."

My eyes traveled glumly around the yard. They came to rest on the treehouse. That's when I had a brainstorm.

"The treehouse!" I exclaimed. "That's the answer! CD can live in the treehouse!"

I climbed the rungs with CD still in my backpack. Tony followed. Then came Ray with the cage. As I lifted CD out of my backpack, he kicked his hind legs. I put him in the cage, careful to fasten the door.

"Max! Dinner!" It was my mom calling.

"I gotta go!" exclaimed Tony.

"Me, too." Ray scrambled down from the treehouse behind Tony.

"I'll be back," I said to CD. "Welcome to the Washington family."

I went inside the house and sat down at the

dinner table. Then I heard my sister yelling from her bedroom.

"Mom!" Tiffany stomped into the dining room holding a pair of socks in her hands. "We must have moths," she said. "The toes are gone in my socks!"

Something had chewed the ends off Tiff's socks.

"Looks like mice," said Dad.

Hulk and Gizmo were at it again.

"Oh, dear." Mom shook her head. "I'll have to get more traps out."

Oh, no! I hoped my runaway pets would stay away from the traps.

As we sat down to dinner, Dad said, "Tiffany, you're not going to wear that hat at the dinner table, are you?"

My goofy sister was wearing her brides-dork hat, as usual. She took the hat off and leaned her elbows on the table. "It's so romantic," she sighed. "Heather loves Dan and Dan loves Heather. I wonder if I'll ever get married."

"Probably not," I said, spooning beans onto my plate.

Tiffany shot me a dirty look. "You baby," she said. "What do you know about love and romance?"

"I know that guys don't go for girls who look like baboons," I said.

Tiffany's jaw dropped open. "Mother!" she exclaimed.

Mom sighed. "Can't we have a quiet dinner?" she asked.

I managed to scoot a roll, some meat, jello, and apple pie into my napkin. After dinner I smuggled it out of the house for CD.

You should have heard Gershwin at school the next day. He sat with us at lunch and started bragging, as usual. Tony, Ray, and I ignored him. But the girls listened. So did some of the other guys.

"Do you really think you'll win the pet contest?" asked Linda.

"I've got a champion dog," Gersh said proudly. "How can I lose?"

Ray, Tony, and I winked at each other. We knew I had a secret pet that would blow the socks off the competition.

Linda leaned across the table, looking at me. "Are you going to tell us what your pet is?" she asked.

"Please?" begged Bev. "What's the big secret? Is it an alligator?"

"It's better than an alligator," I said, with a mysterious grin.

"I doubt that!" exclaimed Gersh in disbelief.

Scott Avery stared at me. "Come on, Max," he said. "Tell us! How can you beat Gersh's champion dog?"

"Easy," I said.

Everyone was staring at me now. The Zimmer-man frowned. He studied me closely. "I think he's bluffing," he said slowly. "I don't think he really has a secret pet."

Bev grinned. "You might be right," she agreed.

"Max made the whole thing up. Didn't you, Max?"

I felt my heart start to pound and my ears grow warm.

"Come on, Maxwell," Gersh said. "Tell us. What kind of secret pet do you have . . . if you have one."

My chest heaved. "I *have* got a pet," I insisted.

"What is it?"

"Tell us!"

"I don't believe you."

"Come on. What is it?"

"A skunk!" I said loudly. "I've got a skunk!" The words just popped out.

Everyone was quiet. They stared. Then they smiled. Then suddenly they all talked at once.

"A skunk? Cool!"

"Neat! You might win the contest after all!"

"A skunk? Wow! Neat!"

Gershwin said nothing at all. He looked worried.

The rest of the day was okay. Not bad for a Wednesday. People came up to me in the halls.

It seemed that everyone had heard about my pet skunk. I just hoped that no one would tell my parents.

I thought about CD all day long. I couldn't wait to see him. When the last bell rang, I hurried home. Before I climbed into the treehouse, I went into the house to change my clothes.

I knew instantly that something was wrong. Tiffany was crying in her room. I could hear her all over the house. She sounded like a smoke alarm.

Oh, no, I thought. *Have Gizmo and Hulk gotten into my sister's underwear drawer?*

Mom and Dad walked into the living room.

"Dad!" I exclaimed. "Why are you home so early?"

"Sit down, Max," Dad said. "We've got some news."

Suddenly I didn't feel so happy anymore. I looked from Mom to Dad. "What's going on?" I asked.

"Max," Dad said, "we're moving to Idaho."

Six

TONY and Ray walked home from school with me on Thursday. I kicked at the sidewalk with the toe of my sneaker.

"I can't believe it," I groaned. "Idaho. They don't even have any professional ball teams there. What's in Idaho?"

"Potatoes?" offered Tony.

"Great," I moaned. "I'm moving to a state where people like vegetables more than sports. I can't believe my parents are doing this to me. Why did my dad have to get transferred?"

Tony and Ray shook their heads sympathetically. "When are you moving?" asked Tony.

71

"As soon as school's out," I said. "I've got one month left."

I felt as if I were going to prison.

"What about CD?" asked Ray.

I sighed deeply. "I don't know," I said. "I want to take him. Maybe I can sneak him into the car."

I wished that my parents and Tiff could move and let me stay in Springfield. I could move into my treehouse with CD. Friends could send food up to me in a bucket attached to a rope. I could move my monster posters in, sleep there, study there, and one day graduate from high school. They'd probably write about me in the newspapers. I'd be known as the Treehouse Boy.

I said goodbye to Ray and Tony. Then I walked the rest of the way home by myself. My stomach did a somersault when I saw the For Sale sign in our front yard.

I could see Tiffany through the front window. She was wearing her goofy brides-dork hat. And there was Mom, still wearing her nurse's uniform.

I didn't feel like being with my family. I'd rather be with a skunk. Without going into the house, I climbed up into my treehouse. CD scratched excitedly at the side of the cage when he saw me.

"Hi, boy," I said. I opened the cage and patted him on the head. When I lifted him out of the cage and put him on the floor, he didn't try to run away. He was getting used to me already. He waddled around the treehouse sniffing at the floor. Skunks sort of rock back and forth when they walk.

"Good boy, CD," I said. I handed him the rest of my lunch, a peanut butter and banana sandwich that I had saved just for him. He loved it.

I remembered how school had gone that day and how everyone kept coming up to me to ask me about my skunk. Others asked if they could come over and see CD. It felt weird to be suddenly popular—and all because of a skunk.

CD finished the sandwich, then licked my

hand. He sure was tame. "I hope you can come to Idaho with me," I said.

"Max! Come here, please!"

It was Mom calling me from the house. She always knew when I was in my treehouse because of the green flag.

I held CD for a minute. Then I put him back in his cage and scrambled down the side of the tree. Inside our house I found Mom standing next to an old lady with gray hair.

"This is Mrs. Hines," Mom said. "She's our real estate agent. She'll try to sell our house for us."

"Great," I said, although I didn't mean it.

Mrs. Hines wore a brown suit. Her hair was pulled tightly into a bun. Her brown eyes seemed to frown at me through her glasses. She didn't seem like the kind of person I'd want to go camping with. Mrs. Hines looked around the living room. "Hmm," she said. "It's small."

The house didn't seem small to me. To a couple of runaway gerbils, it probably seemed like a castle.

I followed Mom as she showed Mrs. Hines around our house. When we got to Tiffany's room, my sister was lying on her bed, reading a magazine about some rock star. His picture was on the front. He had hair down to his butt, and tattoos all over his arms. He looked as if he hadn't eaten since his last birthday.

If that was the kind of guy that girls thought was cute, then I was in real trouble. I wondered if I should get a couple of tattoos before moving to Idaho.

Tiffany jumped up from her bed. Her eyes were red and puffy—either from crying or from gerbils, I couldn't be sure.

Mrs. Hines looked around Tiff's room. "Nice wallpaper," she said approvingly. "This is a lovely, bright room. Elegant!"

Mrs. Hines opened up Tiffany's closet, which was jammed with thousands of clothes that my sister never wears. The box with the brides-dork hat was on a shelf.

Next we went to my room. Mrs. Hines looked

like she was ready to bail out from a wild pitch. She sniffed at the air as if it smelled funny. Maybe it was my gym shoes under my bed.

"Oh, dear," she said, looking at my monster posters. From around the room, veined eyeballs stared and fangs dripped—except for the Headless Warrior, who didn't have eyeballs or fangs.

"I'm afraid that these posters will have to come down," Mrs. Hines said. She walked to my window. "What's this?" she asked, touching the sill as if it had some sort of disease.

Mom looked at me questioningly. "Max?" she said.

I inspected the brown and green lumps stuck to my sill. "Remember when I used to play with soldiers?" I asked. "The window sill was the battleground. Some of the plastic army men melted in the sun."

"That will need to be scraped and painted," ordered Mrs. Hines. She shook her head sadly as she left my room. If she'd had a CONDEMNED

sign, she probably would have hung it on my door.

Next we went to the kitchen. Mrs. Hines snooped around in the pantry. "Oh, dear," she said again.

"What's wrong?" Mom asked. She followed the Mrs. Hines into the pantry, with me close behind. It was a tight squeeze.

I saw what Mrs. Hines was talking about. There on the floor was a trail of sugar. A little corner of the sugar bag had been chewed off.

"Do you have mice?" Mrs. Hines asked.

Hulk and Gizmo were at it again. First it was the lemon pie. Now it was the bag of sugar. It looked as if my runaway rodents had a sweet tooth.

Mom sighed. "I'll get some bigger mousetraps out," she said.

Oh, no! I hope Hulk and Gizmo don't get zapped, I thought to myself.

At last, Mrs. Hines left. Tiffany came

waltzing out of her room with the brides-dork hat on her head.

"At least I get to be in the wedding before we move," she said sadly. "Oh, Mom. All my friends are here. How will I make new friends in Idaho?"

"You won't," I said, "if you keep wearing that dorky hat."

Tiffany stuck her tongue out at me. "At least my bedroom doesn't look like it was hit by a hurricane," she said.

Mom turned to me. "That's right, Max," she agreed. "Those monster posters need to come off the wall. And please take that plastic vomit off the ceiling. I'm so glad that Mrs. Hines didn't notice it."

Take down my posters? Remove the fake barf? Scrape and paint the window sill, site of many cool battles? This was getting serious.

"Clean under your bed, Max," Mom added. "And don't drop your gym clothes around the house anymore. We have to keep the house clean in case someone comes to see it."

"Mom," I said, "I don't want to move to Idaho."

"What?" Mom looked at me.

I felt desperate. "Can't Dad keep his job here?" I asked. "There's nothing in Idaho. People don't live there. Moose live there. Mom, I'm serious. There's a moosehead on Idaho's state flag."

"It's not a moose. It's an elk head," Mom said.

"I don't want to move," Tiffany said.

For once we agreed about something. "All my friends are here," I said. "I like Springfield. This is my home."

Mom sighed. "We're moving," she said. "The decision has already been made. You'll make new friends in Idaho."

I wasn't so sure about that.

The next day was Friday. After school I went up into my treehouse to do my homework. It was one place I could go without someone yelling at me to pick things up or stay clean. It was the kind of place where you could relax with a skunk.

Mom and Dad didn't mind me spending so much time up there because I took my school books with me. I told them that I was doing a report for school on skunks. Which was true. What I didn't tell them was that we had our own real live skunk living in our backyard, eating our dinner scraps, and sleeping in a nest made from our old newspapers.

Studying in the treehouse with CD was fun—except when he ate a page out of my history book. Mr. Lawrence was right. Skunks will eat anything.

CD ran around the treehouse while I worked on my skunk report. As I read, I found out that a skunk's worst enemy, besides man, is the great horned owl. The skunk and owl both hunt at night. Sometimes an owl will dive out of the sky and stick its claws into a skunk. If the skunk is fast enough it will spray the horned owl. That's why some owls stink. This is a true fact, and I put it in my report.

CD crawled up on my shoulder while I read the part in the book about how skunks don't hibernate in winter like other animals. Boy skunks live alone. Girl skunks sometimes live together—sort of like a dormitory in college.

I wrote one whole page, then I took a break and played with CD.

"We're going to win the pet contest, little buddy," I told him. "We'll win the report contest, too. We'll show the Gersh-man a thing or two. That loser thinks he so great. I'll get my picture in the paper so everyone will remember me when I move."

Ray and Tony saw the green flag flying over the treehouse roof. They came over for a while. We tried to talk about Idaho. But none of us knew anything about it. I felt as if my family and I were moving to another planet.

I didn't talk to my parents much that evening. I was still mad about the move. In bed that night, I kept thinking about how everything was changing. My room didn't even look like my room anymore. There weren't any monsters staring down at me from the walls. All traces of a battlefield were gone from my window sill. My ceiling was clean and white, without even a hint of fake barf. It seemed lonely without the dust balls under my bed.

Everything was different. My sister was crying all the time. Mom seemed nervous too. She was trying to keep the house clean, and setting mousetraps everywhere. I was worried about Hulk and Gizmo.

I wondered what would happen to me in Idaho. Would I make friends? Would I get a good teacher in the seventh grade? Would any of the guys love the Redbirds like I did? Would they know that Morgan played on two national championship hockey teams in Buffalo as a goalie before he played for the Redbirds? Would anyone care? Would I be able to smuggle CD to Idaho in our car?

It grew later and later, as I continued to lie in bed and worry about the future. Suddenly I heard a tap-tapping against my bedroom window. Then there was more tapping as raindrops came pouring down. Soon thunder and lightening shook my room. Looking out my window, I couldn't see a thing because of the darkness and the rain.

"CD!" I sat up in bed. My treehouse was dry on sunny days. But it was like sitting in a shower when it rained.

I jumped out of bed, grabbed my flashlight, and tiptoed through the hall and down the stairs. Creeping through the kitchen door, I ran through the backyard. The puddles of rain were cold on my bare feet. Scrambling up the tree, I threw open the trap door. In the light of my flashlight I could see CD huddled in a corner of his cage. His fur was wet.

I quickly grabbed CD from the cage and tucked him under my pajama top. Then I climbed down from the tree and ran back into the house.

In the kitchen I paused to listen. The house was quiet. Good. No one had heard me. Carefully I tiptoed back to my room. I rubbed CD dry with my pillowcase. Then I put him in my closet on a pile of gym clothes.

Back in bed, I tried to sleep. But it was hard because I heard CD walking around in my closet. I'd forgotten that skunks like to run around at night.

I didn't sleep very well. When I woke up Saturday, it was late in the morning and I felt tired. Mom was banging on my door. "Get up, Max!" she called. "Mrs. Hines is showing the house!"

"What?" I jumped out of bed. Through my window I saw Mrs. Hines walking across the yard with a family of dorks. Were these people going to buy our house? Was that boy with the goofy haircut going to sleep in my room?

Mrs. Hines led the family to our front door. I heard CD making hissing noises in the closet.

"Shhh!" I warned him. What could I do?

Should I jump out of my window with CD in my arms? There wasn't time for that. I pulled my clothes on over my pajamas.

"Max? Can we come in?"

Before I could answer, Mom and Dad were in my room with Mrs. Hines and the dork family.

"Max, this is Mr. and Mrs. Snead," Mrs. Hines said. "And their son, Kevin."

As Mrs. Hines walked toward my closet, I jumped in her way. She looked surprised.

"Uh, would you like to see the view from my window?" I asked desperately.

Mom and Dad both shot me a look that said *Get out of the way.*

Mrs. Hines smiled. "We'd like to see the closet space," she said.

Mrs. Snead said, "Storage space is important to us. How large is the closet?"

"Check out the bookshelves!" I shouted. I pointed at my bookshelves, the ones that Dad built. Then I turned to the boy. "Want to see some baseball cards?" I asked. "I've got a couple of Karl Morgan."

Mrs. Hines stepped past me. She looked at me as if she thought I'd suddenly gone crazy. "As you can see," she said to the family, "the closets are roomy."

Before I could stop her, Mrs. Hines pulled the closet door open. Kevin Snead pointed into my closet and shouted, "A skunk!"

Mrs. Hines dropped her papers. "Eeeeeee-eeeeawwwk!" she screamed. Mrs. Snead shrieked. She staggered backward against Mr. Snead, who fell against my dad, who fell against my bookshelf, which fell on the floor.

Mom poked her head in my closet, then suddenly clapped her hand over her nose. CD came waddling out with his tail stuck straight up in the air. Twisting in the middle, he pointed his head and his bottom at us.

Seven

I grabbed CD and held him while Mrs. Snead screamed. Mr. Snead yelled at his son, "Don't touch it! Keep away!" You would have thought I was holding a nuclear bomb from the way everyone was acting.

"Omigosh!" It was Tiffany standing in my doorway. She stared at CD and sneezed. "Ah-choo! Ah-choo! I can't stand it!" she hollered. She looked from Mom to Dad. "First you make me move to Idaho. Then you make me live with a skunk. Ah-choo!"

Mrs. Hines's face looked sort of purple. "I am so sorry," she apologized to the Sneads. "Let's leave immediately!" They practically ran

from my room. The Sneads held their noses even though CD didn't smell.

"He won't spray you," I called after them. "He had his stink glands removed!"

I heard Mrs. Hines's car drive away with the Sneads. CD was in my arms. He gave my chin a lick. I started to smile, but then I saw the look on my parents' faces. I knew I was in the dog house—or the skunk house.

Tiffany sneezed, "Ah-choo! Ah-choo!"

There are times when I wish that I were invisible, that I could walk through walls, or that I could fly to another planet. This was one of those times.

Dad shook his head at me. "Max," he said, sternly, "have you been hiding this skunk from us?"

I thought about telling Dad that I didn't know how the skunk got in my closet. I could have said that I was just keeping the skunk for a friend. Or I could have pretended that the skunk followed me home from school.

Instead I told the truth. I let Mom and Dad know how I felt about the pet contest and how everyone but me had a pet.

"CD's the best thing that ever happened to me," I said. "Can I keep him, please? I promise I'll take care of him. He's real clean. He uses a litter box. He eats cat food or dinner scraps."

"A skunk in the house?" squealed Tiffany. "Oh, Mom, Dad! You wouldn't, would you? What about my allergies? Ah-choo!"

"I'll keep him away from Tiffany," I promised.

Mom and Dad stood there staring at me. Mom shook her head. "Absolutely not," she said.

"I'll be leaving all my friends behind when we move," I moaned. "Can't I take just one friend with me? CD? Everyone at school talks to me now that they know I have a skunk for a pet. It'll really help me make friends in Idaho. I don't know what I'd do without him."

Mom and Dad didn't say anything. They watched as CD snuggled in my arms and rubbed his nose against my chest.

"Please!" I felt like crying. "I won't know anyone in Idaho! I don't want to move. Springfield is my home. I'll be all alone in Idaho. Please let me take CD!"

Mom looked at Dad.

"I'm sorry I lied about having a pet," I added. "I shouldn't have hidden him from you. I'm really sorry."

Dad looked back at Mom. Maybe just maybe they could see how much I needed CD. Maybe they could see how scared I was to move to Idaho. Things were looking hopeful—until my sister jumped in.

"What about my allergies?" she asked. "Do you want my . . . ah-choo . . . eyes to turn red and my . . . ah-choo . . . nose to swell up? Ah-choo!"

"P-l-e-a-s-e!" I begged.

Mom gave Tiffany's shoulder a soft squeeze. "Let's give it a try, Tiff," she said. "I don't think your allergies will be bothered if Max keeps the skunk outside."

Dad looked surprised. "Are you sure, hon?" he asked.

"If the skunk stays outside, then I don't think it will bother Tiffany," Mom said more firmly.

"Mom! Dad! Are you kidding?" Tiffany howled. "Ah-choo!"

"Tiff, the skunk will stay outside," Dad promised. "If you have an allergic reaction, we'll get rid of it." He turned to look at me. "Do you understand, Max? If Tiffany's allergies act up, the skunk has got to go."

I nodded. "Okay. I'll leave CD outside," I promised. "So I can keep him?"

"Yes," said Dad. "But remember, he's your responsibility. And Max . . . ," Dad laid a heavy hand on my shoulder, "no more lying, son," he said. "Understand?"

"Yeah. I understand." CD stretched up and licked Dad's fingers.

"He's awfully tame," Mom admitted.

"Omigosh!" exclaimed Tiffany. "I can't believe

we're keeping a . . . ah-choo . . . skunk.
Ah-choo!" She ran sneezing out of my room.

I spent the rest of the day outside with CD. I
spent most of Sunday with him, too. It felt good
not to be sneaking around. I was glad that
I wasn't lying to my parents anymore. It was
cool to have a pet, at last, even if I had to keep
him outside. What better pet could a guy have
than CD?

The next day at school was Monday. Kids
talked a lot about the pet contest. The contest
and reports were to begin next week.

At lunch I sat with Tony and Ray in the
cafeteria. Linda, Bev, Scott, Curt, and some
other kids sat with us. Then Gersh came along.
He set his tray down across from me.

"Did you hear that Morgan hurt his back
again?" asked Gersh.

"What?" I dropped my hamburger on my
plate. It was just like Gersh to show up with
some bad news.

"I hope he won't be on the disabled

list again," Tony said.

"Is your dog ready for the contest?" Linda asked Gersh.

"Uh huh," he said, nodding. "Mr. Mighty is in championship form. I've almost finished my report, too. Swissies are one of the most interesting dogs around. Long ago the Swissies mixed with St. Bernards. That's how they got to be so big."

I sat up straight in my chair. I was tired of listening to Gersh brag. "They're not as interesting as skunks," I exclaimed. "Did you know that a bear will run away from a skunk?" I asked. "A skunk can shoot a bear right in the eyes with his liquid. He can hit something up to eight feet away."

"That's nice," said Gersh, with a yawn. "Did you know that Swissies were brought to Switzerland by the Romans centuries ago?"

Linda, Bev, and the other kids leaned closer to listen.

"Did you know that the scientific name for

skunk is *Mephitis mephitis?*" I asked. I was glad I'd stayed up the night before reading a skunk book for my report.

"What does that mean?" asked Bev.

"It means 'double stink,'" I said.

Everyone at the table began to laugh. "I'll bet you win the pet contest," Bev said. "Skunks are funny."

Linda smiled at Gersh. "I don't know," she said. "Swissies sound like cool dogs. I think Gershwin will win."

The class seemed to be divided into two groups—those who thought that Zimmerman's Swissy was going to win, and those who thought that my skunk would run away with the prize.

Just wait, I thought to myself. *We'll see if your old dog can beat my skunk. Gershwin and Mr. Mighty versus Max and the Secret Skunk.* It sounded like a wrestling match. Next week would be the final battle between me and the Zimmer-man.

Eight

MONDAY marked the beginning of National Be Kind to Animals Week. Each day in Mrs. Grove's class, we watched and listened as students talked about their hamsters, goldfish, dogs, and cats. Students brought their pets to class on leashes, in cages, and in fish bowls.

Ray told me on Wednesday morning, "I'm going to vote for my dog, Bart. He can eat a piece of bologna off my forehead if I'm lying down. But I think you'll probably win the contest, Max."

"Me, too," said Tony. "Everyone thinks a skunk is a cool pet."

97

"I can't wait to see your skunk," said Curt Daily, walking up to my locker.

"Me, too," said Linda. She stopped in the hallway. "But I still think that Gershwin's dog will win the contest."

I shrugged my shoulders and hoped she was wrong. Then I hurried to English class. Mrs. Grove stood in front of the class. "As you all know, we're celebrating National Be Kind to Animals Week. Today Cheryl Myers will share her pet with us," she said.

Cheryl walked to the front of the class. She carried a cage with a hamster in it.

A hamster. Big deal. So far it looked as if Gershwin and I were still in the lead. I could see the back of his red head from where I sat. After Cheryl, we heard a report from Josh Allamon about his chameleon. It was just a lizard that could change colors. Big deal.

When the bell rang, we all jumped up from our desks. "Hey, Gershwin," someone called. "Are you ready for the contest? I can't wait to see your Swissy!"

The Zimmer-man didn't say anything. He just walked over to the bulletin board where the pet sign-up sheet was. I watched as Gersh took a pen and crossed out his name.

"What are you doing?" asked Bev.

"My dog won't be in the contest," Gersh said. "Mr. Mighty is sick. He's going to be at the vet for a couple of days."

"Oh!" Bev looked disappointed. "I really wanted to see what a champion dog looks like," she said.

"He's really a great dog," Gersh insisted. "He's won all kinds of prizes. He's called a 'Grosser Schweizer Sennenhund' in German. *Grosser* means *greater*. *Schweizer* means *Swiss*. And *Sennenhund* means *mountain dog*."

I couldn't believe it. Mr. Mighty wasn't even going to be in the contest. But the Zimmer-loser was still bragging about him.

"Have any of you ever *seen* Gersh's dog?" I asked suddenly.

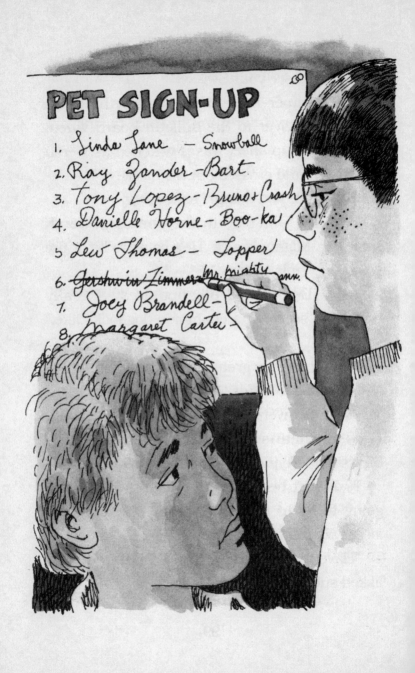

Gershwin stared at me with surprise in his eyes.

"Hmm. Very interesting," I said, raising my eyebrows.

"No one has actually seen his dog. It kind of makes you wonder, doesn't it?"

All eyes turned to look at Gersh.

"Gee, Gershwin," said Bev, "where's your dog? Why hasn't anyone seen it?"

"Why hasn't anyone ever seen your dog?" asked Linda.

"Do you really have a dog?" asked Scott.

Gersh looked embarrassed. He didn't say a word—for a change. He just stared at his feet.

Gersh started talking. "Mr. Mighty won Best of Breed at the Maryland show. Karl Morgan said he wished he had a dog like ours. He thought Mr. Mighty was the best-looking dog he'd ever seen."

No one was listening to him anymore. We hurried into the hall, walking toward the cafeteria. The Zimmer-dork was left behind in

English class. He was probably still bragging to the empty air.

"It looks as if you're going to win the pet contest," Bev said to me.

I grinned and nodded. I could hardly wait! "You'll love CD!" I exclaimed. "He's cool! Did you ever know anyone else who had a skunk for a pet?"

Bev and Linda shook their heads.

"He's real tame," I added. "I've been training him to roll over. He'll do it for a piece of banana."

I'd worked and worked with CD. Most of the time he wouldn't roll over for a banana or even for honey on bread. But he did it once. I figured with more practice he'd get the hang of it.

"I'll bet CD would be worth a lot of money," I said. "Not many people have a tame skunk. I'll bet if they had championship contests for skunks, CD would win."

My friends floated around me like a cloud as I walked down the hall.

"Does he bite?" Bev asked.

"Nah!" I said. "I'm not afraid of him. A wild skunk will bite. Even some tame skunks will bite. But not CD. Anyway, he's had his rabies shots."

Turning to Tony, I said, "Dad got some front-row seats for the Redbirds game. He said we could go to a few before we move."

"Front row?" asked Tony.

"Yeah." I grinned. The company Dad worked for had given him the tickets.

"Excellent!" exclaimed Ray. "Front row!"

"You know, I'll bet even Karl Morgan never had a skunk for a pet," I said. "He probably just had a dog or a cat."

Cheryl carried her hamster cage as we walked along the hall. "I wish I had a skunk," she said.

"Max, are you really moving to Idaho?" asked Bev. "That's so far away."

I shrugged. "Yeah. We're moving. Mom says we're going to get a house with a swimming pool in Idaho. We'll get a bigger house, too. Not like the little, dinky ones around here. Maybe I can get a dirt bike, too." Actually, Mom had never mentioned getting a swimming pool or buying me a dirt bike. But she did tell me that Dad was getting a raise, so it didn't seem like too big of a stretch to think we might get some cool stuff after we moved.

Taking a deep breath, I said, "I can't wait for Friday. My picture will be in the paper, for sure. CD will win the pet contest no problem! My report is great, too. CD is the coolest pet there is. I'll bet no one in this school has ever had a skunk for a pet before."

No one said anything. Tony and Ray were looking at me. They had the same look on their faces that *I* had the first time I met Gershwin Zimmerman.

Nine

GERSH didn't sit with me at lunch that day. Neither did Tony and Ray. I couldn't find them in the cafeteria. I couldn't find Tony and Ray after school, either. They were acting weird, so I walked home alone. I saw the Zimmer-man walking on the other side of the street, going in the same direction. He was alone, too.

When I got home I found Tiffany in the living room with Mom. Tiff was wearing her brides-dork dress and hat. Mom was sticking pins into the bottom of the dress.

Tiff looked like she was going to a Halloween party. Usually I would have joked with her—asked her where she parked her broom. But today I didn't say anything. I had too much on my mind. I was thinking about Ray and Tony and how suddenly they didn't seem to like me very much.

Mom looked up when I walked in. "Mrs. Hines is showing the house in half an hour. So don't make any messes."

"Yeah," said Tiffany. "And don't let that skunk near my dress. Omigosh. If Tammy sees skunk hair on my dress at the wedding, I'll just die!"

Mom stopped pinning Tiff's dress and said, "That's it for now." My sister went to her room.

Mom stood up and looked at me. She patted my shoulder and said, "Let's talk, Max." Mom sighed. "Honey," she said, "your Dad and I have decided that we won't be able to take CD to Idaho with us. It just won't work out with a skunk in the car. I hope you'll understand."

"What?" I couldn't believe what I was hearing. "You're kidding! Leave CD?" I asked. "Can't we take CD and leave Tiffany?"

Mom shook her head. "I'm sure you can find

a good home for CD here in Springfield. Maybe Ray or Tony can take him. You can get a new pet after we move, something that can live outdoors."

"But, Mom!" I exclaimed.

"I'm sorry, Max," Mom said. "It's just not practical. It's a very long drive. It would be hard for CD. It would be impossible for Tiffany."

I jumped up and stomped off to my room. "Max?" Mom called. I didn't answer her. What could I say? No one ever listened to me anyway.

I went outside to see CD. At least someone was happy to see me—even if it was a skunk. I didn't care if he got skunk hair on me. I let him out of his cage. He licked my hand and rubbed his nose against my chest. "Hey, little buddy," I said, patting his head. "How are you?"

CD seemed even more special than ever. It felt like everyone else was either mad at me or bossing me around. It was just me and CD. I thought of a hundred things I could do to keep him—run away with CD, join a circus, mail him to Idaho in a box, or sneak him into our car when we moved. But I knew none of those things would work.

It wasn't fair! How could I give CD away? Which one of my friends would take the best care of him? Tony or Ray?

CD waddled around the treehouse while I sat on the floor, watching him, and thinking.

"What will it be like in Idaho?" I asked. CD looked at me the way he always does when I'm talking to him. It's like he's trying to understand me.

"How will I make friends?" I asked.

I thought about Gersh and how he came to our school and made friends by bragging. He talked about his house, his dad's pet store, his mother the model, his autographed baseball, and how Karl Morgan came over to dinner.

I didn't even know whether or not the things he bragged about were true. I'd never seen Gersh's dog. Neither had any of the other kids. How could we know if Gersh's dog was real or not, when none of us had ever gone to his home?

Wow! The thought hit me like a beanball—right between the eyes. I remembered how embarrassed Gersh had looked when I asked him why no one had ever seen his dog. *We hadn't seen his dog because none of us had ever gone to his home.*

Gersh never got together with the guys to wrestle and ride bikes and belch and laugh and trade baseball cards. He bragged to people, but getting people to listen to you wasn't the same as getting them to like you. I should know. Everyone listened to me talk about CD and how I was going to win the pet contest, but Ray and Tony weren't walking home from school with me anymore.

CD jumped on a bug in the corner of the tree house and ate it. Then he swished his black-and-white tail across my hand.

I patted CD's head and kept talking. "It must be hard to be the new kid in town. I guess bragging is just one way to try to get into the crowd."

I remembered all the things Gersh said about his dog. How Mr. Mighty was rare and expensive. How he was strong and smart and well-trained. How he won contests and ribbons. How he was better than everyone else's pet.

Gersh's bragging made me want to barf. But still, it was clear that Gersh loved his dog. He loved Mr. Mighty as much as I loved CD.

Whoa! I felt like I got hit in the brain with another beanball. It was weird. Maybe Gersh and I had something in common after all.

CD pushed his little nose against my hand, searching for food. I ran my fingers along his back and down his fluffy tail. Suddenly, I knew what I had to do.

"Good-bye, little buddy," I said.

It was after school on Thursday when I finally got the guts to go through with it. Mrs. Zimmerman answered the door. I was surprised at how tall she was, but then I remembered that Gersh said she was a model.

Mrs. Zimmerman looked from me to CD.

"I'm Max Washington," I said. "I go to school with the Z-z- . . . with Gershwin."

"Hello," Mrs. Zimmerman said. Then she called over her shoulder, "Gershwin! You have a visitor!" Gersh came walking into the hall carrying a book. When he got closer I saw it was a book called *History of Greater Swiss Mountain Dogs.* He shrugged and looked embarrassed. "It's for my report," he said.

Mrs. Zimmerman opened the door wider and I walked in, carrying CD in his cage. CD ran nervously around, poking his nose through the wire mesh.

Gersh stared. "Is that your skunk?" he asked.

"Yeah." I nodded.

"Cool!" Gersh knelt on the floor to get a better look. Then he said, "Bring him into the kitchen. The light's better in there."

I followed Gersh and his mom back into the kitchen. It was big and smelled newly painted. I saw a dog dish on the floor, but no dog.

There on the kitchen table were papers, pencils, and more books about Swissies.

Gersh looked embarrassed. "I haven't finished my report yet," he said. "I'll have a report tomorrow, even if I don't have a pet."

"It's a shame Mr. Mighty is still at the vet," Mrs. Zimmerman said, sympathetically.

CD pawed at the side of the cage.

"Can I hold him?" asked Gersh

"Sure," I said.

Gersh opened the cage and lifted CD out. CD stuck his tail straight up in the air. But as soon as Gersh began to pet him, CD calmed down. He even licked Gersh's hand.

Gersh petted CD's head. "Cool pet," he said. "You'll win the pet contest tomorrow, for sure."

"No, I won't," I said. "You will."

"Huh?" Gersh looked puzzled.

I never knew before that smiling could hurt. But this smile did. I looked at CD in Gersh's arms. "He's all yours," I said.

"Wow!" Gersh looked as if he'd just won the

World Championship. He stroked CD's bushy tail. Then he looked at me. "Why are you giving him to me?"

"I can't keep him," I sighed. "Now that we're moving I have to find a new home for him."

Gersh's blue eyes stared at me through his glasses. "But why me?" he asked. He acted like I was trying to play some kind of trick on him.

I didn't feel like talking anymore. It hurt too much. CD didn't understand what was happening to him and I felt bad. I looked at Gersh. "Don't you want him?" I asked.

"Of course I do!" Zimmerman smiled and petted CD's head.

Mrs. Zimmerman stared at the skunk.

"He's tame," I reassured her. "He's had his rabies shots and his musk glands removed. He doesn't stink."

"We'll need to talk with your father," Mrs. Zimmerman said to Gersh. "Let's see what he has to say about it. He should be home pretty soon." She glanced at her watch.

Gersh put CD back into his cage. Then he grabbed a banana from a fruit bowl on the kitchen table. Peeling the banana, he gave a piece of it to CD. CD started munching on it. Bananas are one of his favorite foods.

"I've gotta go," I said.

"Can I keep the skunk tonight to show him to Dad?" Gersh asked his mom.

"All right," Mrs. Zimmerman nodded.

I gave one last look at CD. He was too busy eating the banana to notice when I left. It was just as well. I didn't want him to be sad. Gersh walked me to the front door.

"Thanks," he said. "I'll take good care of him. I promise."

"Okay," I answered. I've never been one for making long speeches. I knew Gersh was the best person to take CD. He knew a lot about animals because his dad owned a pet shop. Anyone could see that Gersh was nuts about Mr. Mighty. He was sure to go double-nuts over a cool pet like CD.

I walked down the sidewalk with a mixed-up, happy-sad feeling. Happy for Gersh. Sad for me. I went home. There was that For Sale sign in our front yard. I didn't feel like going in my house. So I climbed into the treehouse.

It wasn't the same without CD. I missed him running around the treehouse, climbing over my leg, eating snacks from my hand, listening to me. It was awfully quiet. I sat there and thought about Idaho. I'd be the new kid. I'd have to make it on my own now. I wouldn't have a skunk to pave the way for me.

The silence was suddenly broken by the sound of screams. Yelling and shrieking came from my house. It sounded as if somebody on the FBI's Ten Most Wanted list was chasing my family.

As fast as I could, I scrambled down from the treehouse. The screams grew louder as I neared the house. Throwing open the kitchen door, I ran inside. The noise was coming from Tiffany's room. I raced through the house.

Mom, Dad, and Tiffany were staring into Tiffany's closet.

"My hat!" screamed Tiffany.

I pushed Tiff aside. There was her hat box on the closet floor. Inside the box was the brides-dork hat with its mess of ribbons and flowers. And there, in the middle of the hat, were two gerbils and four gerbil babies. The babies were tiny and pink. Their eyes weren't open yet.

"Hulk! Gizmo!" My two gerbils looked up at me. I reached into the box. Hulk ran up my arm and sat on my shoulder, just like I'd taught him to do.

"Eeeee-awwwk!" screamed Tiffany. "Ah-choo! Ah-choo!"

Mom and Dad looked at me. I tried to smile. "They're mine," I admitted.

I never suspected that my gerbils were planning to move into Tiffany's hat. It never occurred to me that Gizmo might be a girl. Who'd have thought that Hulk and Gizmo were

married—or whatever it is that gerbils do?

"Can I keep them?" I asked Mom and Dad. "I could take them to school tomorrow for Pet Day. I don't have CD anymore. I gave him away. Can I keep the gerbils, just until we move? Please?"

"Ah-choo!" Tiffany blew her nose. It sounded like air going out of a balloon.

Mom sighed. Dad shrugged his shoulders.

"Okay," Mom said. "But, Max, you'll have to keep the cage in the basement. And you'll have to find a home for them before we move."

"Omigosh!" Tiffany wailed. "What about Heather's wedding? Ah-choo! I can't wear a hat with rats on it!"

"They're gerbils," I corrected my sister.

Tiffany glared at me. "First it was a skunk," she said. "Now it's rats. Just look at my hat!"

Gizmo and her babies were lying comfortably between a silk rose and a velvet ribbon. Not a bad home for a gerbil.

Ten

"**YOU** did what?" Ray and Tony asked me the next day at school. They couldn't believe it.

"I gave CD away yesterday," I said.

"Why didn't you give him to me?" asked Ray.

"Max, are you having a nervous breakdown or something?" asked Tony.

I sat at my desk with Hulk in his cage. Gizmo was home with the babies. If you ask me, Hulk was glad to get away for awhile. He nibbled on seeds and ran in the exercise wheel.

Gersh sat at his desk with CD in a cage on the floor. Everyone in the class was gathered around him asking him questions about CD.

When the bell rang, Mrs. Grove read names from the attendance sheet. Then she looked from me to Gersh. "I'm confused," she said. "I thought that you had the skunk, Max. Gershwin, wasn't your pet a dog?"

"I'm giving a report on a skunk," I explained. "But my pet is a gerbil."

"I'm giving a report on a dog," said Gersh. "But the skunk is my pet."

"Oh. I see," said Mrs. Grove. But she didn't look as if she saw at all. "Let's begin," she said. "Gershwin, would you like to go first?"

Gersh read us a report about Greater Swiss mountain dogs. He showed us some pictures of Mr. Mighty in the competitions that he had been in. He was black and white, with tan legs. He had a big chest and looked strong.

When Gersh was finished with his report, he took CD from his cage. "This is my pet," he said. He flashed an embarrassed grin my way. "A friend gave him to me," he added.

Everyone looked at me. Now it was my

turn to be embarrassed.

When Gersh was finished, I walked to the front of the class with Hulk in his cage. First I read my report on skunks. I told the class about how a tame skunk is friendly and smart. I told about how a skunk hisses and stamps its feet when it's angry—sort of like my sister, Tiffany. I told them that skunks like to eat at night—sort of like my dad.

"CD used to sleep in my lap," I said. "His favorite drink is milk mixed with eggs and honey. Most skunks stay wild, even after they're tamed. But CD is different. He doesn't bite."

As I talked, CD began to run around in his cage. He saw me standing in front of the class. He knew my voice. I knew that with time he would get used to Gersh. He would love Gersh just as much as he loved me.

After my report I showed the class Hulk, who did his trick of climbing up my arm to my shoulder for a piece of cheese.

Then the voting began. Mrs. Grove passed

around pieces of paper with all the students' names listed on them.

"I'll tally up the votes," Mrs. Grove said. "We'll have our winners by the end of the day. The newspaper reporter will be here to take the pictures of our two winners and their pets."

Everyone started talking at the same time. "Gershwin's going to win," Bev said.

"Gersh has got the best pet," Linda Lane sighed. "He'll win for sure."

"I'm voting for my dog, Bart," Ray said, loyally.

"I'm voting for the Zimmer-man," Curt said.

"Me, too," exclaimed Scott.

"Me, too," I said. How could I not vote for CD?

We marked X's by the pets and reports we liked the best.

Gersh sat at his desk, smiling. He reached down, poked his fingers through the cage, and petted CD. At the end of class, his mother came to take CD home. I tried not to think about it.

The rest of the day seemed to drag by slowly.

Gersh sat with us at lunch. We talked about the Redbirds and how Morgan came back from an arm injury. He slid into first base on an infield single. Even though he was hurt in May he hit eight home runs in June. There's a guy who doesn't give up. He could probably make the best of anything—maybe even a move to Idaho.

When school was finally over, the sixth-graders rushed to read the winners posted outside of Mrs. Grove's classroom. There it was:

1st Place—Most Interesting Pet—
 Gershwin Zimmerman

1st Place—Best Report—Max Washington

"It's a no-hitter! CD won everything!" I exclaimed.

"What a great skunk!" Gersh agreed.

"You guys get your pictures in the paper," sighed Linda. "You're lucky!"

We went into Mrs. Grove's classroom, where she was waiting with a photographer from the local newspaper. I held Hulk in his cage in front of me. Gersh and I stood together as the photographer took our pictures. His camera clicked and flashed again and again. I felt like a movie star. Someone like Karl Morgan is probably used to getting his picture taken, but not me. I'd never won a prize or had my picture in a newspaper before. It was cool.

When it was all over and the photographer was gone, Mrs. Grove said, "Good job, boys." She smiled at us as we walked out into the hall where Ray and Tony were waiting.

I grabbed my gym bag from my locker. Hulk was in his cage, under my other arm.

"Here," said Gersh. "I'll carry that for you." He grabbed my gym bag.

The four of us—me, Ray, Tony, and Gersh— walked home from school together that day. We lived near each other, and it was time we got to know Gersh better. After all, it's not easy being the new kid in school.

Gersh asked me about Idaho. "What's it like

there?" he asked. "Any professional ball teams?"

I shook my head, sadly. "Nah," I said. "I'll have to watch the Redbirds on TV."

"You'll come back to visit, won't you?" asked Tony.

"You better," said Ray. "My dad will get us Redbirds tickets if you come back."

Good old Ray and Tony. I thought about how it sure is hard to leave your friends behind when you move. It's sort of like being a ballplayer who gets traded to a new team. Maybe Karl Morgan will feel this way some day if he leaves the Redbirds. Maybe he'll start a professional ball team in Idaho. And maybe not.

"I hope the kids in Idaho aren't snobs," I said.

Gersh nodded his head. "Just be yourself. Don't be a showoff. Just act normal."

I couldn't help smiling when I remembered all the showing off that Gersh did when he first came to our school.

At the corner we stopped. With a grin at me, Gersh said, "Thanks again for CD. Maybe I can pay you back sometime."

"Forget it," I said. "Just take good care of him. He's a great skunk."

Gersh nodded in agreement.

Ray, Tony, and I had a quick belching contest. That was always a nice way to end a school day. Tony won, as usual. Gersh just watched.

"Bye," I said. "See you guys tomorrow."

Gersh handed me my gym bag. With my gym bag in one hand and Hulk's cage under the other arm, I walked home. It was hard to carry all that stuff. I was almost home when I felt everything starting to slip out of my arms. Quickly, I put Hulk's cage on the ground. Then I dropped my gym bag. It tipped to its side. As it hit the ground, a ball came tumbling out.

The ball rolled into the grass and I picked it up. It was a baseball with writing on it. I read the words:

Good luck wherever you go!
Karl Morgan

About the Author

Janet Adele Bloss lives in Ohio with her husband, Ron, and two children, Matthew and Suzanne. When Janet isn't writing, she likes to play with her kids—climb trees, stomp in mud puddles, and go on flashlight hikes at night.

Janet says, "When people read my books, they're getting a peek into my daydreams. It's fun to share my dreams. I love writing for kids because they have such great imaginations."

Janet visits schools and talks to students about writing. She sometimes gets ideas for her stories from the kids she talks with. "If I'm going to write for kids, I need to hear what they have to say," she explains. "Kids might be little, but their ideas are big!"